CAT
IN A CORNER

For Eleanor, William and Bernie

with love

J.L

ORCHARD BOOKS
96 Leonard Street, London EC2A 4RH
Orchard Books Australia
14 Mars Road, Lane Cove, NSW 2066
Text © Hiawyn Oram 1996
Illustrations © Judith Lawton 1996
First published in Great Britain 1996
First paperback publication 1997
The right of Hiawyn Oram to be identified as the Author
and Judith Lawton as the Illustrator of this Work
has been asserted by them in accordance with the
Copyright, Designs and Patents Act, 1988.
A CIP catalogue record for this book is available
from the British Library.
1 86039 169 9 (hardback)
1 86039 431 0 (paperback)
Printed in Great Britain.

CAT IN A CORNER

The story of Robertson

Hiawyn Oram

Illustrated by
Judith Lawton

ORCHARD BOOKS

Read about your favourite animals in these other Animal Heroes...

Dog in Danger
The story of Sidney and the Hedgehogs

Dolphin SOS!
The story of Nemo and Lemo

Monkey in Space
The story of Chi

Robertson, the marmalade cat,
was visiting.
He was visiting
his owner's mother
while his owner was away.
He hadn't stayed with her before
but he wasn't complaining.

This was a woman
who knew how
to treat a cat.
She'd built him
a roaring fire
and placed
a soft, plump sofa
right in front
of it for him.

Her cooking –
served on fine china –
was the best
Robertson had ever tasted.
And the rest of her family
treated him as if he was –
which of course he *was* –
the most beautiful,
intelligent, sensitive,
deserving, marmalade cat
in the world.

"Love it, your ladyship,"
Robertson purred.
"Love the house.
Love the family.
All up to scratch.
Now what about
the garden?
Mind if I take a look?"

Robertson padded
out of the kitchen door
and round the side of the house.
"Well, I'll be mouse-trapped!"
he gaped.

He was standing
on a vast lawn.
Beyond that was
another vast lawn.
Beyond that was a lake –
a small lake
but certainly
a fish-filled lake.

And beyond that
woods and fields.
Hunting grounds
as big as the world.
"Hmmm,"
Robertson mewed.
"Very much up to scratch!"
He set off across
the first lawn.

How deliciously alive it felt.
And wasn't that
the smell of rabbits...?

He marked out
some stone steps
for sunbathing
and moved towards
the lower lawn.

And then...
there it was...
right in front of him.
Oh bliss! Oh heaven!
Oh all his birthdays
and all his Christmases
rolled into one...
A BIRD TABLE!

A large bird table full of birds –
surrounded by birds
feeding greedily
on food that had
fallen to the ground.
Robertson's eyes focussed.
His body froze.

It couldn't be helped.
It shouldn't be helped.
It had to be done.
He slunk,
he streaked,
he POUNCED!

And what a dead-eyed pounce!
His mouth was full of it –
fat, feathery wagtail.
"Brilliant!" he rejoiced.
"I shall present it to her ladyship
as a thank you
for having me to stay!"

Ignoring the other birds
swearing at him
Robertson swaggered
back to the house
and laid the bird
at his hostess's feet.

"Robertson!" she screamed.
"How could you? How could you?
You bad, bad, bad cat!"
"Bad cat?"

Robertson was shocked.
Were they speaking
the same language?
Surely she meant good cat,
great cat, fantastic,
dead-eyed pouncer cat?
"Sorry," he mewed.
"But I don't speak
mumbo-jumbo."
Then with head held high
he strolled into the
sitting room
and jumped on to
her husband's lap...

to enjoy being treated
as if he was
the most beautiful,
intelligent, sensitive,
deserving, marmalade cat
in the world.
"Which of course I am!"
he purred...

…when he woke the
next morning and
smelt his breakfast cooking.
"Fresh, buttery kippers!
My favourite,
your ladyship!"

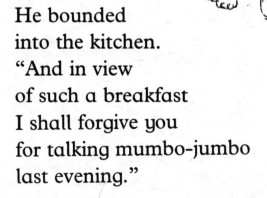

He bounded
into the kitchen.
"And in view
of such a breakfast
I shall forgive you
for talking mumbo-jumbo
last evening."

After breakfast
he sat on the kitchen steps
and washed himself.
"What a beautiful day
in every way," he sighed.
"I think I'll take a look
at the lake..."

He padded off
across the upper lawn
and down the stone steps.
And then –
there it was again.
It hadn't moved.

That bird table
full of birds –
surrounded
by birds –
peckers and gobblers
and feasters.
Robertson's eyes focussed.
His body froze.
It couldn't be helped.
It shouldn't be helped.
It had to be done.
He slunk,

he streaked,

he POUNCED!
His mouth was full of it –
fat, feathery
goldfinch!

"Just as it always
should be!" he rejoiced.
"And this time I present it
to no one."

Keeping to the flowerbeds
he slunk back
across the lawns,
into the house,

and buried the bird
under the dining room rug.
"Ha, ha!" he mused.
"No one will find it here...
though I say it myself,
'Good work, Robertson!'"

Then putting on his
completely-innocent-face,
he went into the hall to sit
in a patch of sunlight and
keep guard with one eye
and snooze with the other.

"Robertson!
Robertson!"
It was her ladyship
disturbing him
and she was *furious*.
"Robertson!
Where have these
feathers come from?
You've done it again,
haven't you?"

26

"Done what?"
Robertson
hurriedly licked
a feather
from his nose.

"You've caught
another bird.
You have! You have!
I know it!"
"Bird?
I see no bird,"
mewed Robertson.

As she was clearly
about to start talking
mumbo-jumbo again,
Robertson decided
to go upstairs
and sleep
under a bed
until she came
to her senses.

When he woke up it was dark
and he was starving.
"Strange...she must
have forgotten
to call me for supper."
He hurried downstairs
to see what was on the menu.

"Not up to her usual standards!"
Robertson sniffed.
"Tinned, if you ask me!
And served on a plastic plate!"

Still, he was so hungry
he couldn't help
eating up every scrap.

Then feeling the chill
of the dark, empty kitchen
he strolled into
the warm sitting room
and jumped on to
the sofa to enjoy
being treated
as if he was...

But what was this?
As he sat down
her ladyship's
husband got up.

Without a word.
Without even a
'Good evening Robertson'.
Robertson sidled along the sofa
to the girl-relative.
"Prrrr..."
He butted under her hand.
"It's me, Robertson.
Most beautiful..."

But she too got up
without so much
as a 'Good evening'.

Robertson sat on
the edge of the sofa
and looked over
at her ladyship
reading in an armchair.
He mewed.
She didn't look up.

He mewed again.
Nothing. Not a flicker.
"Probably a little deaf,"
Robertson mused.
"Poor old thing."
He leapt down
from the sofa...
and rubbed
against her calves.

But no hand came down
to scratch him.
He jumped on to the arm
of her chair.
She ignored him.

He nuzzled her ear.
She ignored him.
He slid down
under her book
on to her lap –
and she not only stood up...

she tipped him onto the floor,
picked up her book
and walked out of the room!

Robertson couldn't believe it.
It wasn't possible!
How could they IGNORE
the most beautiful, intelligent
sensitive, deserving
marmalade cat
in the world...
unless...

unless...
it was something to do
with that bird...?

He hurried to the dining room
and turned over the corner
of the rug.
Nothing there!
He tried the other corners.

Nothing there either!
Could her ladyship
have found it?
Was that what this was all about?
He sat down to think.

Maybe, he thought,
'bad cat for catching birds'
meant – in her ladyship's language –
'cats who catch birds
will be completely
and horribly
IGNORED...?'

Robertson wandered
back to the dying fire.
He curled up
close to it
and sighed deeply.
If he was right and he knew he was,
there was only one thing for it.
And tomorrow he would have to do it.

And so the next morning
after he'd eaten
a tinned breakfast –
served in stony silence
on the plastic plate –

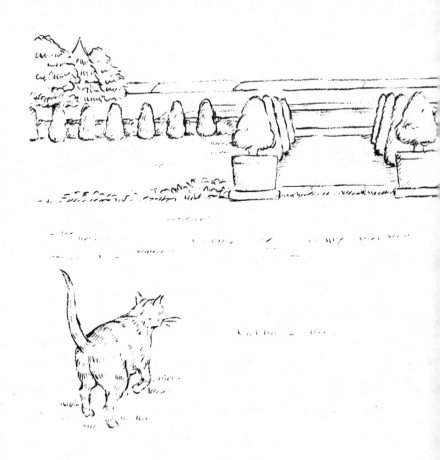

Robertson padded out
of the kitchen door.
He padded across the upper lawn
and down the stone steps
to the lower lawn.

And there it was.
Right in front of him.
The bird table!
The large bird table
full of birds –
surrounded by birds –
peckers and gobblers
and feasters!
His eyes glazed.

His body stiffened.

It should be helped
but it couldn't be helped.
It had to be done.

With a huge effort of will
Robertson walked slowly
and calmly over to the bird table...
curled up under it,
and slept.

CAT IN A CORNER
is based on the true story
of an English marmalade cat
who went to stay with
a bird-lover and had
to be taught – somehow –
NOT TO TOUCH HER BIRDS!
The author has changed
the names of any people
and put words into
Robertson's mouth.

Here are some other Orchard books about animals that you might enjoy...

PIPE DOWN, PRUDLE!

1 85213 766 5 (hbk) 1 85213 770 3 (pbk)

RHODE ISLAND ROY

1 85213 764 9 (hbk) 1 85213 768 1 (pbk)

WELCOME HOME, BARNEY

1 85213 765 7 (hbk) 1 85213 769 X (pbk)

WE WANT WILLIAM!

1 85213 763 0 (hbk) 1 85213 767 3 (pbk)

A FORTUNE FOR YO-YO

1 85213 583 2 (hbk) 1 85213 679 0 (pbk)

SLEEPY SAMMY

1 85213 584 0 (hbk) 1 85213 677 4 (pbk)